I0630158

Published by LaCarey Entertainment,LLC
P.O. Box 41354 Washington, DC 20018

Manufactured in the United States of America

Dedication

To every woman, it is because of you I exist. I love you
with the deepest compassion and honor that I am able to form.

I hope I am able to give you warmth and
pleasure as you read my book.

Thank you for sharing life with me.

Table of Contents

PAGE

In The Hallway	1
Ummm	3
She Got What She Wanted	5
On Your Ankle	6
BBW You Have Done It Again	9
Erectness	11
Damn Woman	12
Fresh Out Of The Shower	14
I Would Prefer If You Ride	17
Size Doesn't Matter	19
Teaser	22
The Reason I Want A Son	24
The Taste Of Your Absence	25
The Right Woman	27
Your Peak	29
A Reason To Smile	31
Awaken Something Inside of You	34
I Am A Lucky Man Indeed	37
Comfort Zone	40
Promise Tomorrow Will B Like This	42
Searching For Your Love	44
Are You A Booty Call	47

You Had Enough?	50
The Way You Want It	52
What Would I Do Without You?	54
Your Sweat	56
Wow	58
What Would The Readers Think	60
Be Better Than Her Last	62
Who's Going To Be There?	65
Something To Show You	68
Queen	69
Look At Me	70
Hey	71
Can I Part You?	73
For No Reason	74
Just A Résumé	75
On Nights So Cold	76
Keep Begging	77
Celibate	78
April Shower	80
Freaky	83
Following After A Tragedy	85

In The Hallway

Your apartment is three doors away...

But we can't make it.

Ripping my pants open like you're going to take it...

I am waiting.

Eyes closed.

The warmth of your palm makes him roam

Around in your hand until you take control again.

Three doors away...

But right here is where I want to be.

So sweet,

The joy of the hottest space and feeling no teeth.

You got me

On my tippy toes.

Hands opening and closing...

Body roaring.

And it turns me on to know that you are enjoying

Three doors away...

You look at me

Eyes beyond earth,

Looking into mine to monitor your worth.

Lowering your lips and skirt.

This feels so good that it hurts.

Lift you by holding you up by your legs

On the fourth step they spread.

Panties tugged to the side as I lower my head.

Your upper body leans back...

Three doors away but we ended up on the steps.

Ummm

Ummm…

This is the first decision that I made that was right.

The rest of my life

With you.

I do.

You do.

We do.

Love you.

Forever.

Together.

Ummm…

Ummm…

It makes me giggle.

To know that I will always be with you.

This made everything else worth going through.

I am here with you.

Sharing each other's first breath of the day.

And every last breath of the night you choose to breathe on me.

Ummm…

Ummm…

I am so pleased

For you to grant me all that I will ever need.

You.

Hell yeah! I will always do.

Love you.

Marry you.

Ummm…

Ummm…

She Got What She Wanted

She said I made her panties wet

So she gave them to me.

All I ever wanted was her heart

But, I took what I could get.

Sent her home with a memorable limp

And my scent

But not my embrace,

My kiss,

My lick.

The things she didn't think she could get...

And I never put it all the way in.

On Your Ankle

Stand there pure,

With no words,

You are enough just to see,

You have me

Behind your left knee.

Kissing.

Licking.

So soft.

I caress my cheek against you like a cloth.

I love you inch by inch.

Every particle of you is meant

To be this way.

Look at me.

Aroused by the thickness behind your knee.

Pre-cumming...

You do this to me.

Regardless of where I touch,

I always lust.

You turn me into flames.

Caressing...

Licking...

Kissing...

This very spot

And knowing it is your body part has me so hot.

Breathing heavy.

Touching you as often as you let me.

A slave to your pleasure

As long as I can claim that we were together.

I will leave with less of me than I came with

But carrying more of you away in me.

Can you feel me shaking?

Without touching myself,

I feel like ejaculating.

I want to thank you.

Leaving my desire all over your ankle,

You just blew me away.

Now I just want to curl up at your feet

And sleep.

Hoping to record, in my dream, you walking away from me

So I can rewind your pace

And close my eyes at will and hear you coming to me.

BBW's You Have Done It Again

Big Beautiful Woman

I'm still enjoying the after taste.

Licking my fingers trying to recreate…

Thick chins, wide waist, and an ass that always shakes.

I get up close, like right before my face.

You keep me feigning…

Like when you put those legs in the air and open wide, always has me beaming.

We make love with the lights on…curtains drawn.

And I am harder than any porn you can pick.

You got me like this.

Not because you are thick…

But because you are on the most wanted BBW list.

Oops, did I just drip?

They don't believe you can ride on the tips of your toes.

A skinny chick ain't got a thing on you.

And when you let your back side loose

Count down before I shoot.

Overwhelmed with your affection,

You have to keep your panties on for protection.

Unless I get freaky...

Slide them to the side and let our ending do it leaking.

You, I can't get enough of.

That thing fits around me like a glove.

Best I've ever had...

So if you are not what the world considers over weight, I'll pass.

I like lots and lots of ass...

Lots and lots of legs...

Lots and lots of waist line...

Because that always leads to a big ole' behind.

Call me your mystery man

Because I am going to creep up on you every chance I can.

And of course, I love you.

How could I not?

You are a BBW.

Erectness

I stand there holding the flames of erectness.

Wanting to add to the chain of your desire.

There is blinding comfort in our haze but I walk toward you anyway.

Needing to feel the heat of your splash.

Swimming inside your crimson.

I turn blue.

I turn red.

I turn in circles wanting to grab hold of my emotions

but then there was the explosion.

You chose to catch the sparks with your lungs.

I remain silent.

I remain content.

At least for twenty more minutes.

Damn Woman

All day I have been walking around with this

thing pressing against my jeans.

"Freedom," it seems to scream.

Or is it release?

I wonder what it would say if it could speak.

For no reason, you cross my mind and it jumps.

My mind scans your body and it jumps.

So I focus just a minute…

Then my mind jumps from your shoulder to your center.

Head gets larger because now I am about to enter.

I catch myself grabbing my print.

Snatch my hand back, for this is forbidden.

But my mind will not let my eyes see.

It's like you're standing in between my focus.

He's doing his own thing because my jeans keep on poking.

And I know he is swollen

Cause I can feel the veins

Through my jeans

And I ain't touching a thing.

It's like your hands are caressing upwards on my legs

And he's begging to be eaten or fed.

And I still can't find my focus.

The wetness between those thick thighs got me

damn near choking

But I am hoping to change my thoughts.

He's done got so long that he got himself caught...

Is it mine, his, or your fault?

But now he's stuck.

So I unbutton my jeans and lower my zipper to get him up

And he jumped right in my hand.

Damn...

Woman, you got me again!

Fresh Out Of The Shower

Fresh out of the shower,

Sitting on the toilet and drying off with a towel.

Where did you come from?

Your eyes covering your naked body

asking me did I want some?

Didn't have a chance to answer...

Legs thrown over mine was your answer.

Gripping the back of my head,

The other hand steadies me from in between your legs...

Lips finding my head.

Pressed against me...

Feeling like you eased into me.

Slow rise.

Widening of your thighs.

Slow fall.

Leaving only the dangling of my balls.

~ 14 ~

It's your fault that it's lost.

You rise with ease

Reminding me that I don't want it free.

Your pace quickens.

After the throbbing, it seems to thicken.

My lips, you're licking.

So delicious.

Refusing my kissing.

Throwing your head back like you wanted me deeper in it.

Neck gripped with both palms.

I lift your legs with my arms.

You want it deeper.

This should make it much easier.

My skin feel delighted against your breathing.

You pause...

Quickly standing and pinning your back against the wall

But your lower waist drop.

You whined as if you are seeking me to pop.

Don't stop!

You rise to the tip before a quick thrust.

Putting you down, just remembered you like it rough.

Spinning you around to the front

Steadying myself to enter your ass.

I Would Prefer If You Ride

What if I ran my fingertips across there?

Around your thighs until running beneath your pubic hair.

You know, those same thighs that you say are too thick.

What if I planted a kiss?

No, I want to lick

So you could understand that the extra thickness

Makes me get thicker quicker.

So quick that you felt the need to grab and stroke my it.

What if I let you hold it as I glide my palms up your sides. . .

The stomach line that you despise?

That same spot you said is too much extra meat.

What if I decided to lick and suck that stomach

that you don't want to keep?

What if I asked you to drape those arms around me that you say are too flabby?

Parting your soft cheeks and pulling you closer as you grab me.

Hold me so near that I can whisper into that neck you say you are losing.

What if I told you I love the way it rests against base of my tongue,

would that be confusing?

At the same time, my attention just thrust up and over your clit.

Now the length is pressed against it.

The swollen tip rests against the stomach you want to forget.

You felt it sway and almost drop.

Only landing in your hand because its fall you wanted to stop.

You still felt the need to stroke...

Staring in my eyes and neither of us spoke.

Breasts so delicate that I held one and lost the nipple of the other in my mouth.

Teasing it with my lips, sucking it in and out.

What if I dropped beneath you wanting to rub those knees

that you say are wearing down?

What if I started kissing beneath them as I make my way downtown?

Would you stop me because you say you don't like your body?

I have one question, now that you are deciding...

I would really prefer if you would ride me.

Size Doesn't Matter

Somebody said that size doesn't matter.

That was until the head got in and throbbing made it fatter.

That was until it stopped at the entrance

And allow your wetness to reveal everything you were thinking.

Or was it when I got half way in and stopped…

And you whispered that was further than any other man had got.

Or was it when two inches were left and eight inches were gone…

Is that when you realized that you were wrong?

See, size doesn't matter.

So tell me why I am not moving and you keep getting hotter?

See, a doctor would think that your body was overheated.

So I raised your legs to make travel easier for your releases.

See, size doesn't matter.

So I pump slowly because speed is not what you are after.

And I don't give you all of me

Because size doesn't mean a thing.

But I can hear your imagination

And I can feel from the tug from your lips that you're tired of waiting.

Your hips no longer rock, they thrust.

So I pull the head all the way out before I begin my thrust.

I heard you curse

And felt the intensity from your first squirt.

See, size doesn't matter.

So I being all the way in is not a factor.

See me reaching for your bladder

But painting your walls as I make my way doesn't matter.

Tell me, what are you after?

Because I can feel it coming through my veins faster.

So I increase my pumps

And swipe every spot that you want.

And still increase my pumps,

Pushing to the end of me to crumple your grunts.

If size isn't want you want,

I'm going to change your mind.

Flip you over and enter from behind…

But still taking my time.

So tell me, what you are after…

If it is not length or thickness?

As long as you can cum, the size becomes insignificant.

Teaser

I don't know what was on her mind.

I woke up and all I could see was her behind.

Cheeks spread and feet planted firmly on the bed.

She had risen all the way to the tip of my head.

The length of me was soaked with her juices.

No need to run from me now so I thrusts

upward with no excuses.

She grabbed my ankles tighter.

So I grind inside of her just a little nicer.

She looked over her shoulder with eyes wild with lust.

She mumbled something like "Don't be gentle.

You know I like it rough."

So I sped it up.

Pump after pump.

Spreading her cheeks…I played with her asshole with my thumb.

She's in a zone.

~ 22 ~

She's yelling now. No more moans.

I slid up until I was on my feet.

Doggy style position...pussy lips the only thing holding me.

So, I dig deeper.

Grinding.

Clockwise...then counter.

Slid him halfway out and thrust him back in just as a reminder.

Standing on my tippy toes with my balls on her back.

She likes it like that

Cause I am curved to the left.

One hand palming her shoulder

And the other gripping her hair

Before dropping my lower body under her cheeks

just to get deep in there.

Pressed against her so tightly that every time I grind to the left

That lip opens a bit...

And spits.

The Reasons I Want A Son

I wanna take you to your mother's house

And fuck you under the roof where your father pays rent.

I want to experience your creation to its fullest extent.

I don't mean any disrespect.

I want to cum where your mother gave your father consent.

The birth place of greatness...

And I lack the patience.

Tossing your panties to the side so there will be no waiting

And I will control my pacing

Until it reaches the speed

To loosen my knees.

Release so powerful that I know one of these will

produce a seed.

I can feel this is the one.

My only prayer is that we have a son

Cause I would hate for my daughter's man to try to repeat this one.

The Taste Of Your Absence

The taste of your absence

Leaves me captive…

Captivated

And making love to the images that are not before me.

Mentally so turned on

That I caress myself like you used to.

Smelling your pillow.

Lost as if I was kissing you.

So stimulated.

So erect.

The hair on my neck searches the atmosphere for your

Lips…

Fingertips.

So I'm hard.

So hard.

It lifts.

So I sit up.

It rises

Waiting for you to take a seat.

I'm missing you

So much.

Your touch.

I'm wet.

The tip.

Mentally watching you sit.

I can't help it.

I grab it.

The Right Woman

Destiny whispered her design for me after licking my earlobe.

Fate told me after her third orgasm that rough times will prepare you.

And pain remembered my name when I loved her harder.

An angel wrote to me that God gave me freewill...

just remember to respect your father.

See...but love opened the door for me when I

became committed to her needs.

And you...you made the good times and the bad times the best times in my life.

And even though fate, destiny, and pain,

even the angel didn't tell me that you would be my wife.

But see, the higher power saw fit.

That without trials and tribulations, my time with you

would only blend in with other sensations.

So he kept me waiting.

Forcing me to learn patience.

I had to experience hatred

To understand broken hearts are only part of the equation.

He knew that you were a queen.

I had to be built into a king.

But a king can't oversee a thing

If he knows nothing.

So I had to learn not to talk about myself but to hear something.

That's when it hit me.

That's when I realized you were standing in front of me

the whole time but were a mystery.

Learning life on life's terms.

But part of a higher plan.

No man really understands.

That the best thing you can have in life is the right woman.

Your Peak

I welcome you...

I welcome you with open arms long enough to touch

in spots that you crave to be felt.

See, I will be the release that awakens you to your peak.

Then I will carry you over until you spill for me in splashes.

And I will hold you...

Soft but firm and close to me.

So close to me that my flames will jump in between your kisses.

Then I will swallow you...like you're the connection to my life or death.

My tongue will flicker in between each heartbeat to increase your lust.

See we are in tune.

I will touch you with hands that don't have palms

But they know your curves.

I will trace you...with the outline of my erection.

Then I will cum not before you or after you...but with you.

So that we will melt into each other like pleasure is supposed to.

Then I will wait for you...to tell me what you need from me.

And I will stand in two places, if need be, to make sure your needs are met.

And if you only need for me to just rest...

I just ask that you allow me to look into your eyes.

So my dreams will know I am not willing to leave you here.

A Reason To Smile

I want to put my ear to your heart to hear your orgasms.

And stick my tongue in between your muscle spasms.

I want to be part of your release

And find new ways of pleasing you like slowing licking underneath your feet…

Or behind your knees…

Or go so deep in you that it feels like you are seeing things.

I want you to find my hands locked against your flesh.

Tongue circling underneath your breast…

Fingers sliding down your spine…

To open your behind…

Lie myself in between your cheeks…

Ear against your back to listen for the popping of your release…

Or tickle you between both holes.

Watching your fingers stretch then fold.

Inside, the tip of me goes.

You breathe.

Sounds like you are losing your ease

Or grip on patience.

Only interested in giving you a few inches.

For the others you must do some waiting.

Your body begins shaking.

Fingertips creeping up the back of your neck.

Your hairline starting to sweat.

Then I find a grip.

Pull your hair just a bit

Before inserting a little more than the tip.

Do you think you can handle this?

Your cheeks ease back.

Stilling a half of another inch.

This is a shame.

I turn it up by whispering, in your ear, my name.

The same thing you were thinking.

Easing your shoulder forward now you are bending.

And I throb

Glancing at you trying to stroke the rod.

Yes, it is so hard.

My mind racing.

Now I am impatient.

Thrusting harder inside,

You thrust back and enjoy the ride.

I just smile.

You are not as nice as you believe.

You are a little wild.

Awaken Something Inside Of You

You stand there naked in the dark.

Legs spread apart

Above me.

I inhale.

Indian style I sit in between your walkway...

Speak to me.

Palms setting my fingertips free.

They begin caressing...

Reaching...

Needing.

Fingertips brushing the bottom of your sweet cheeks

Only to glide down below your knees,

Stopping at the inner sides of your ankles.

This is how making love is supposed to be.

Slowly.

Kissing below your left knee,

Fingers and palms gliding

Over the front and back of this leg.

Kissing you there.

Caressing you there.

Grip tightens.

Tongue pressed against you lightly

Before leaning backwards for the other leg.

Fingers stroking as they spread.

You feel good.

No longer wanting to wait.

Now tongue and leg meet.

Long slow strokes.

Doing this slowly.

You need to know I will find pleasure in every part of you.

I am so hard for you

That he bangs above my belly button.

Splattering desire of wanting

But I cling to you.

Fingers more aggressive

They press and slide as my knees part.

Head tilts back in the dark.

Mouth open.

Tongue still soaking.

Head rising.

Tongue widening.

Fingers open you.

Tongue and your wetness soaking you.

I Am A Lucky Man Indeed

I found you seated at the table asleep.

I tiptoed just to take a peek.

I went to kiss the top of your ear.

Being so close made it clear

That my kiss would turn wet.

You stirred revealing your neck…

I kissed

From your neck back to the top of your ear.

Awake now because soft moans I can hear.

Palms holding your shoulders.

Too excited…now touching myself I have become swollen.

You read my mind.

Reaching from behind.

You touch me and I pressed against your hand.

Deeper kisses above your ear.

I could hear your stomach turn.

So I know this is your spot.

And if I slipped my fingers down I would find that you are wet.

But instead I turn up the heat by kissing your shoulder.

You moan louder, coming closer to me.

I am free because I could feel the warmth of your hand stroking me stiff.

Gripping your shoulder harder…

Licking your shoulder then neck.

Your head drops back as you jerk me into submission.

Flooding the top of your ears with my kisses.

I can feel my veins

Sing in between your pumps.

I grunt.

I want you now.

I want you bent over the table.

Thrusting inside of you until we both are unstable

But instead you turn in your seat

Taking me deep in your mouth…never felt your teeth.

Kissing your shoulders that I hold still with my grip.

Before pre-cum could surface, you swiped it.

Licking your lips to let me know my taste you like it

Gripping the top of your hair…

Trying not to go there.

Madly sucking and licking the top of your ear

Down to the back of your neck,

Your moan meets mine.

Holding your ear between my lips trying not to lose my mind.

You pump me as you swallow the head.

I am starting to lose feeling in my left leg.

You inhale and the strokes are so smooth.

My grip, hold, cum, I lose to you.

You push the seat back

And lean over the table and snatch your cheeks back.

I am a lucky man indeed.

Comfort Zone

You crossed my mind several times since I've been away.

So, I am sending you this just to say

You are inside of me

Where I feel your presence anywhere I shall be

And you feel good traveling across my mind.

Comfort, for the most part of my life, was a struggle to find

So I thank you

For making me feel at home...

And never alone

Inside myself.

And I am well aware that I can reach out of me for your help

So I feel safe.

And I just hope when I am away

That you also feel me inside of your space.

It's nice to have you enter my private zone.

I can hear your footsteps

And laughter when you enter my dome.

Good to be home.

So take off your shoes.

I just wanted you to know that I never leave home without you.

I felt your lips around me

Pulling me out of my mind.

I had to grip your hair to maintain nothing.

You are good at everything...

That makes me blush.

And I love you even more

For these moments.

When words escape us both

Your actions

Leaving me reacting.

I plan to return love in the same form.

Promise Tomorrow Will Be Like This

Today you meet me at the front door with a pair of lips

That I kissed

Until the day disappeared.

When reality hit me again, we were on the stairs.

Your leg up, back against the wall, my hand locked and

gripping the back of your hair

Making sure that I am all the way in there

Just like you like,

Right in the middle of the flight

Of stairs

You rode me there.

All lips wet.

Drinking your kiss.

Feeling your hole split.

Deeper I get.

Your tongue flicks.

I'm grinding up against your clit.

So wet.

My whole morning is gone.

Life breathes love in your arms

Underneath your grip.

My tongue in between your lips

Before disappearing in between your hips.

Promise tomorrow you will greet me like this.

Searching For Your love

Did I tell you how life could never love you enough?

So I try to help you feel love through my touch.

You mean so much to the falling and rising of my thoughts.

You make me squirm on the inside

And my orgasms are the only evidence I can't hide.

So, I cling to you...

Drinking the very being of you.

So you keep cumming

And I will catch every drop until you stop running.

Then I will hold you within my chest

Or arouse you with the tip of my tongue against your breast...

Starting with the left...

Gliding to the right.

Unless you go, I will find love in you all night.

Fingers clinched against pressed palms

As your lower side rises to the tip of my throne.

I will move...inside...you are home.

You make finding love a thrill

And I am pleased that we can both refill.

So cum!

You can have all you want...

Until enough is enough.

And I will journey through any opening you want.

So tell me where to find love in you

So I can apply the needed pressure

Whether it is inside of a closet

Or on the edge of your dresser.

Rest your ankles against my shoulder

And I will search for love for you...

Beneath all lips...

Through every hole and split...

Whether I use fingers or lips...

Or the print...

That is so visible.

It vibrates because it can hear you.

Looking for love

We'll leave wet spots

Next to your puddles.

Or if fortunate, we'll cum together.

I'll find your love...

Searching your past memories to give bad times a hug,

I promise this.

Covering every layer of your body so I won't miss it.

I have one question...

All of this?

Or would you prefer I just read a book to you?

Are You A Booty Call

I love it when you call me over

And immediately request that I move closer.

Smile as you grab my hand...

No need to saying nothing.

Fingers finding their way under my shirt.

The fire in your eyes leap instead of lurk.

I'm naked...

You're naked...

On the couch.

You were on top of it before I knew it was out.

Every wave must fall.

Sinking in and hitting all walls...

So wet.

Your lust is so hard to forget.

But I meet your every thrust

Until your back rises then I push.

Your arms thrown back

Picking up your bounce because you like it like that.

You lean back further so now I am curved.

You must have known that I was on the verge.

But you kept control.

So I swing up toward you.

Gripping you harder than I adore you.

Dropping you onto your back.

No need to ask you knew what was next.

Palms clenched to the edges.

Pass seven inches, you stopped begging.

You thrust.

I thrust.

Legs locked behind my legs,

Pulling back until I see the head.

Then I dive

Back inside...

In between your thighs.

Another inch lost inside.

Your eyes close.

Tongue exposed.

Insides explode.

I whisper in your ear...

I gotta go home.

You Had Enough?

It's slippery.

It's wet...

Nudging it upward with my nose.

Then my tongue thick, wide, and wet runs over it...

Flickers against it...

Seals the top with a kiss.

Then a suck.

Tongue flickering back and forth.

Holding it at the base.

Sucking.

Lips tighten their grip.

Tongue slipping and sliding

Around the base.

Slowly

Lips release you.

Tip

Of tongue

Glides slowly up and down the sides.

Your wetness mixed with mine.

Tongue flickering so fast that it out races time.

Lips hold and suck.

Tongue vibrating.

You fully stimulated.

Lips release.

Back of tongue gliding across the top...

Then stop.

Lips lock.

My tongue pulls against the sucking of my lips.

Fighting for your clit.

Miss,

You had enough?

The Way You Want It

I want to draw you a picture...

The moon rests softly on the deep smooth sky.

The air is cozy as if you set it to your comfort.

I can hear the waves humming a sound so seductive

That water kisses your heels.

Tropical fish pluck pearls onto the shore

Because your love speaks in languages that vibrate from your existence.

The world makes sure you never need.

You are love.

You are loved

So much that the sand licks your flesh.

Your nakedness is at home.

Your body feels the desire of the world.

Now you ache to express your feelings...

Licking your lips to caress the air.

It kisses you back, but it's unfulfilling.

You dig the back of your fingers into the sand to hold its desire

But it slips through your grip.

You cast a look of longing to the moon but it smiles back.

How good it is being loved.

If you can not give it back

Then I'll rise up from beneath the tropical fish.

Holding only my desire in your gaze.

This is how love was meant to be...

Shared.

Naked on the beach

The way you pictured.

What Would I Do Without You

This is what makes it hard for me to stay focused…

I love you deeply and I thought that you completed me

But my cravings have increased.

You have awakened something inside of me that I named my freak.

Now I find myself lying with this other women between her sheets.

But I love you…so I touch Tonya with the lights off.

And I never put my tongue where her panties fall.

But she's so soft.

So before and after having sex,

I use my tongue to clean her off.

See I would never betray you by holding her chest together and

Suckling her breast with the caress of my tongue.

See you're the one whose thighs I leave moist

So I hold her from the back and that's really her choice.

And it amazes me how two women can claim me at the same time.

So I part myself in two. And when I am with you…

I love you

And when I am with her…she's my boo.

So my message to both of you…

What would I do without you?

Because you make me whole.

Your Sweat

I'll taste the sweat that flows from you

Only so that I'll have something you can never take back.

I wanna lay my soul beneath your flesh

And place my thickness in the spot of your wish.

See, I want you to be filled with me.

I want your body to teach my body how to be soft by your thrust.

I only want my soul to witness for us

Because I promise

I will be as attentive as you need me to be.

See I will let my hands be free

And just allow my waist to dictate.

Until you tell me to relax the muscle in my face

And eat.

I will until you scream you are complete.

Then I will reinsert me

Until your body has a release that can't be denied.

I want you to cum until your eyes are dry.

I will cry until I water you again

And ask my soul have I sinned. You are holy.

And I only want to pleasure you to a level so divine

That my mind screams your name in its own voice

To a point that we both speak at the same time.

And love is ever so present that my soul caresses your spine

While I kiss you between your breast.

I want to experience elevating our sex

Until we take flight.

There is no need to say I love you.

I just want you to experience cumming for the rest of your life

In any position that you like

With any part of my body that you chose.

I just want to be used as your tool.

So from my limbs…To your hot spots,

I remain your dildo with no batteries attached.

So use me.

Wow

My back still stings from your kisses that snatch skin and instill desire.

My screams match yours as your body rises higher.

I never knew that you could fly

Or make me mentally reach the sky.

I cum inside myself never wanting you to stop

So I motion to allow me back on top.

My touch is yours.

My experiences are yours.

My favorite person is you...

All because of what you say and do.

You keep promises that never lie.

Sometimes your touch is so overwhelming.

With glee, I ask God why.

If I am a fool,

I will lose

Again and again

Underneath your touch

In between your thighs

Gripped in your palms.

I explode wherever you choose to touch me

Awake or asleep…

You have turned me into your freak

And I fucking love it.

Discovering myself in you.

What Would The Readers Think

Love is so hard to find.

Most of us chase this image throughout our lifetimes.

People say be patient

Because love is part of your destination.

I fall deeper in love during the waiting.

Just to taste her bottom lip...

To find someone with matching fingertips.

To hold her, time skips...

Every time I see her neckline.

My fingers travel her spine.

Kissing beneath her hair trying to read her mind.

But I already know

Because her lips always say," I love you."

How wonderful it is to be standing in this space...

Occupying it with one that will make everyday a blessing.

To love without rules.

Combining our being together so smooth that

we don't know our differences.

You are your own person.

And I still remain me.

But together we create something stronger that lasts longer than lust...

More overpowering than our lack of trust.

Heaven redesign humans because of us

And when we lust

Our insides touch.

While our flesh waits for us to come back

We define...opposites attract.

You're my lifeline and I am yours back.

Now I wonder after reading this...

What would the readers think

If they find out you're white and I'm black?

Be Better Than Her Last

She told me that in order for me to make love to her that

I would have to be better than her best.

Then she told me

This was the first time he used the key.

The same key that told him no wall shall separate him from me.

I was lying on the couch half asleep.

No panties.

I touched myself an hour ago with all fingers.

Palms planted.

Clitoris standing

Until I drained me.

But I still wasn't free

So I went to sleep.

Now he's hovering above me...

Smiling.

Running his fingers along my mind,

At the same time raising my spine.

Then he kissed me.

Licked me.

Gripped me.

Pulled me into his mouth.

Even if I wanted to, I couldn't shout.

Wetness painted my thighs.

Oh, I thought I was too dry.

His fingers and hand did glide.

He gripped me at the same time parting my lips so his fingers could get inside.

Damn!

I wanted to swallow his hand

But instead I set his zipper free

And the other prisoner fell over onto me.

I bathed him through my teeth

But he wouldn't know I had teeth.

I moaned.

Before I knew it, my mouth was empty and he was gone.

But inside my walls he appeared.

Gripped his back! Fuck that gripped his head.

I could feel my own wetness pulling at him every time he went deeper.

My back arched. Womb thrust forward begging him to keep her.

So I grind against him.

His balls banging against my lips like they miss him.

I felt it throb so I knew what cumming was.

My mind trying to grab something...

But he stopped.

So did my heart.

Kissed me around my neck until he was behind me.

Still kissing me

And soon, still filling me

The way we both like.

Who's Going To Be There?

Who's going to keep your heart...

When your mind falls in love?

Who's going to feel the pain...

When your heart begins to hurt?

Who's going to love you like you do...

When you need to be loved?

Who's going to take care of your needs...

When you need in a hurry.

Who?

Who?

Who's going to be there for you?

They say that we all have somebody for us.

But how many times do you think you have found?

Even when you give your all,

You seem to be let down.

So who's going to tell you when you're right?

The mind plays many games,

And your heart reaps all the pain.

So who's going to love you like you do?

Who?

Who?

Who's going to be there for you?

Many times our thoughts are puzzled

And we are so confused.

Who's going to tell you your thoughts for you?

Who's going to hold your hand?

When you need it to be held?

Who's going to tell you things that you can't tell yourself?

Who?

Who?

Who's going to be there for you?

Many say they can love,

Many can even try.

Things were never meant to fall.

Why are the tears leaving your eyes?

Who's going to tell you why?

Who's going to be there?

Who's going to care?

You need somebody real,

So be still,

Until I get there.

Something To Show You

I will keep in mind…eternity.

But we must be going to hell because there is something burning inside me.

I bring you to me in the center of the boat

And with my teeth I remove your clothes.

God must have remembered what I like…

Because he gave you to me as my wife.

As you hold me close

I use my fingers to open the back of you…

The crack of you.

You are so soft; I slide around to the back of you.

Ride my erection along the slit.

But this will be romance so I won't rush to it.

Shit…

I am geeking to be enclosed inside of you

Feeling your juices riding me boo.

Queen

Her body is her castle.

I only dream of worshipping within her temple.

Inspire song through the lungs of her choir.

I want to bath her heart under candle light with kisses.

Read to her thighs underneath her waistline.

Hold the doors to her opening wide so rain can pour out.

Then I want to fuck her until the castle losing all power.

We fall to sleep in dream land.

My finger in her...

Her hand around me...

Just in case one of us wakes up.

Look At Me

I understand your waistline and that sometimes you feel

like that's your biggest crime.

And I know how just touching that spot, just right, can make you unwind.

See I don't understand when you say your weight is an issue

Because I'm thinking all day that I can't wait so that

I can hold you and kiss you.

Woman you don't realize how bad that this man can miss you.

I'm talking about waistline to thigh.

See, I knew that would make you smile

Because you know I'm talking legs high...mouth open.

Hey

For no other reason,

I run my hand over the softness of your flesh

Trying to swallow my lust

Over your feet.

My urges increase…

My body speaks…

So I creep.

Calves so fit.

The back of your ankle I press against my lips.

This is deeper than desire.

This is fire.

My lips crawl

Below my palms

To the back of your knees.

Now my palms sweating.

My imagination showing me that you're wetter.

Right there where I know I'll find my blessing

But I must exercise patience.

So turned on that I'm debating.

So I refocus and press my cheek against your flesh just

to catch your pores opening.

You feel so good.

Your body heated.

You just don't understand how bad you're needed.

So I caress my way along your thighs.

You open wide.

I smile...

I may be here for awhile.

Can I Part You?

Can I part you? I want to get so into you

That I brush against you everywhere I turn.

That I have no choice but to turn you on.

But see, that is my desire.

Get so deep into you that I am able to take you higher.

Lift you where your mind and body meet.

Just by me touching...

A little brushing...

A lot of thrusting.

But touching you...being inside of you...

Between all of your feelings...

Slowly bringing you to a point that you have to speak what you have been shielding.

And when it comes, it is so revealing.

My touch can be healing

If you are willing.

Can I part you?

For No Reason

Hunger and lust control my emotions...

with you running rapidly through my mind of the night before.

I search for you.

Longing for you.

I hear the tingle of a fork or knife in the kitchen.

My heart beats faster of the thought of your lips against me.

Pulling me into you.

Your lust is greater than my desire.

I see you standing there in booty shorts and my body becomes fire.

You turn to me. Your eyes trace my erection.

You smile before looking into the camera lens.

I set it where it can view you.

View us. Tonight I'll cover you with your thoughts of passion

and increase that with my desire to master your satisfaction.

You make me hard for no reason.

Just a Résumé

I am more than just a résumé.

The things you see are only small particles of me.

I am determination in the flesh.

And I use every inch of my body so don't hold your breath.

Never give anything less...

Than my best.

Whether it is in the streets...

Or in between the sheets...

I bring the heat.

So if u choose to go any further

Brace yourself...

You are about to experience me.

On Nights So Cold...

You were caught in the chill.

You said I warmed your body....

Just thinking I was there.

Keep Begging

It would be my greatest pleasure just to leave the head in

Just for the games you like to play.

I'll have you begging...

Swollen.

If you're tied up there are no restrictions to the holes I'll go in.

I'll make it quick

And as slow as it can get

But you will only get the head and not the length...

Just to keep you begging.

Celibate

I saw you from the glow of the computer screen.

Your beauty just gleams

And you look so soft.

I signaled you by a cough.

You glanced over...consumed by Yahoo Messenger

But said, "Yes, sir?"

Now, that was my queue

Whether or not you intended to.

Slipped up behind you...

Your shoulders are so smooth.

Kissed you on the corner of the right one

Then I bit you because I wanted to taste some.

That turned into a lick

That traveled over to your neck.

You leaned back with your eyes closed.

Over, around, and consuming your left nipple.

Pulling my lips back...tip of tongue on the center.

Hand by your mouth then you begin to lick my fingers...

So I leaned into you.

Lips gripping the nipple...the back of my tongue sucking you.

Leave one and flicker against the other

Gripping them both with my hands like a jealous lover.

Pinning them together...

Sucking the nipples together.

Tongue slips underneath...of each

Circling them...

Feeding off of them.

You kept your eyes closed.

If they were open you would have to say, "No,"

You're celibate.

I am so ready that this is relevant

Because it will not bend.

So I slipped him in between the twins

You know...just to keep you celibate.

April Shower

I am lost.

Searching through your pleasure places…

Trying to find your release.

You are divided here.

Everything I find, I am pleased.

But until you release

I search you…

Behind the G-spot…

Over the clit.

Taking my time,

Not wanting to over look a thing

But taking pleasure in bringing you closer.

I found love here.

I found pain here.

I found my name here.

And I had no clue that I was here.

Only you, I knew

And your name echoed through my touch.

Outside of the walls, I search...

Not sure if your release was behind or under your lips.

So I suck here...

Lick there...

Nibble there...

Still I'm not finding.

Taking my search around the clit.

Slowly underneath I track you.

From left to right, I glide...

From top to bottom, I try to find...

Before, taking you inside.

No release

But a lot of moving.

So I am close.

Back to the G-spot, I go.

You are soaked...

But not enough.

So using fingers, I apply an additional touch.

I feel your back raise up

Sweeping around the walls my name comes back up.

I rediscover love and a pain

And mixed them with my name.

Faster my search goes

Penetrating with my fingers.

Nose inhaling your clit.

Touch searching faster.

You scream a higher power…

And the release poured into me almost like an April shower.

Freaky

She stooped before him.

His erection cradled and rocked softly in the palm of her hand.

She batted her large eyes at him to signal her comfort.

Her lips inhaled the beginning of his hardness as he blew

out the pleasures of her warmth.

She worked him with long slow strokes while popping

the head in and out of her mouth.

Every few seconds she would stroke him upward while

staring up into his eyes.

She desperately fought back her smile.

This was easy.

She knew if she swallowed he would be hers for life.

"Daddy. Daddy. She moaned.

He looked down at her with a calmness that only confirmed her belief.

"Huh." He forced himself to utter.

"Are you going to cum in my mouth." She pleaded.

Immediately, he squirted and splattered cum all over

her eyes, nose, chin, cheek, and mouth.

She didn't miss a beat. She swiped some of the cum off of her

cheek with the tip of her tongue.

Then she smiled up at him as she rose.

She kissed him and scrapped the cum off the top of his mouth

before pulling away.

Following After A Tragedy

Following after a tragedy,

Fingers locked above our heads.

Tongues forcing the other's to the depths of a kiss

Into the rain…

Under a tree.

Maximizing our wetness

By our fantasies.

Thunder opens the sky

As you open for me.

And I harden against your breast.

In front of the neighborhood…

In front of the noisy neighbors…

A block from the house…

I don't care.

Too caught up in my zipper to break us free

You look good.

Dress up around your waist.

Back against the trees,

Leaning into me...

I, into you.

Fumbling to free your breast with steady hands.

Two forms of wetness against your nipples.

Two forms of wetness on my fingers.

One beating.

The other pouring.

I love this shit.

Until your left leg rises and rests over my right thigh

Now I praise this shit.

Feel like I am floating inside.

I thunder inside as the sky crackles

Into you.

Loving you in rage

Near the tragedy.

Where I tried to break up with you

And you with me

One of us asked for one more experience

But this is a U-turn in a relationship

That will never be stable.

To Contact Baby Oil:

LaCarey Entertainment, LLC
Attention: Baby Oil
P.O. Box 41354
Washington, DC 20018
Email: oohbabyoil@yahoo.com
Web: www.oohbabyoil.com

OTHER CREATIONS BY

LACAREY ENTERTAINMENT LLC

IMAGINE
A Spoken Word CD By Lamont Carey
Available from LaCarey Entertainment, LLC.

To hear some of the tracks on the CD go to:
www.myspace.com/spokenwordpoetry

To purchase the CD, visit: www.lamontspov.tk

LAWS OF THE STREET
Laws of the Streets" is being filmed in Washington,
DC as a TV series. It is a humanistic view of those who
live life according to the laws of the streets. It goes
past the sensationalistic headlines that trumpet the
crime de jour to the behind the scenes "WHY" of life
choices made and desperation of those involved

Please visit: www.lawsofthestreet.com

LAWS OF THE STREET ON STAGE AT THE
J. F. KENNEDY CENTER
This is a LIVE taping of a shorter version o f the TV series being
performed as a play at the Kennedy Center. The play and TV series
was written by Lamont Carey. Spokenword was used to narrate
the play.

For additional information, please contact:
www.lawsofthestreet.com or
lacareyentertainment@yahoo.com

OTHER BOOKS RELEASED BY

LACAREY ENTERTAINMENT LLC

WHY I KEEP U A SECRET By Lamont Carey (available)
This is a poetic view of relationships from a guy who never knew love as a rose. The passion, the pain, the lust, and the hope in love can be felt with every word. Love doesn't hurt between soul mates.

Please visit:
www.lamontspov.tk
www.lacareyentertainment.com

REACH INTO MY DARKNESS By Lamont Carey (available)

This book of spokenword/poems is about struggle, fear, conviction, hopelessness, survival, determination, and triumph. It contains the lyrics from Lamont Carey's most popular spokenword pieces such: *Confidence, I Love My Son, I Hate This Place*, and *The Streets Keep Calling Me*.

Please visit:
www.lamontspov.tk
www.lacareyentertainment.com